Lincoln and Grace

Why Abraham Lincoln Grew a Beard

BY STEVE METZGER
ILLUSTRATED BY ANN KRONHEIMER

Scholastic Inc.

Photo Credits:
page 11: "Proclamation of Freedom to Millions!" Rare Book and Special Collections,
Library of Congress; page 20, top: Votes for Women ribbon, Rare Book and Special
Collections, Library of Congress; page 20, middle right: Suffragette Parade, Library
of Congress; page 20, bottom right: Suffrage flag, Library of Congress; page 32:
Inauguration of Mr. Lincoln, Library of Congress; page 40, middle left: Abraham
Lincoln Portrait, Library of Congress; page 40, bottom right: Lincoln and Grace
Bedell sculpture, Don Sottile.

Text copyright © 2013 by Steve Metzger
Illustrations copyright © 2013 by Ann Kronheimer

All rights reserved. Published by Scholastic Inc. SCHOLASTIC and associated
logos are trademarks and/or registered trademarks of Scholastic Inc.

ISBN 978-0-545-48432-9

12 11 10 9 8 7 6 5 4 3 2 1   13 14 15 16 17 18/0

Printed in the U.S.A.   40
First printing, January 2013

Many people consider Abraham Lincoln to be the greatest president in the history of the United States. Today, when we see images of Lincoln, he usually has a beard. That's one of the reasons he's so easy to recognize.

On pennies:

On $5 bills:

At the Lincoln Memorial:

And on Mount Rushmore:

Why did Abraham Lincoln decide to grow a beard?
It all began with a young girl. . . .

In the summer of 1860, eleven-year-old Grace Bedell lived in Westfield, a small town in New York. There were seven brothers and sisters in her family. . . and a baby on the way.

Grace enjoyed shopping for clothes with her mother, decorating her dollhouse, and playing Blind Man's Bluff with her friends.

"I'm going to get you!" Grace called out.

Family dinners were fun for Grace, except when the discussion turned to the upcoming presidential election. That's when she first heard about a tall, relatively unknown candidate — Abraham Lincoln.

"I think Lincoln would make a fine president," Grace's father said. "I agree with his position on banning slavery in any new states that join the Union."

"I disagree," said George, one of Grace's brothers. "I'm going to vote for Stephen Douglas."

"Me too!" said Levant, another brother. "Lincoln's a clumsy backwoodsman who doesn't know anything."

"I wish I could vote for Lincoln, too," Grace's mother said. "But, unfortunately, I can't."

"It's not fair that Mama can't vote!" Grace said. "She's as smart as any man."

"Grace, who do you think should be our next president?" George asked.

"Well," Grace replied, "if Mama and Papa like Lincoln, I like him, too."

"Why don't you think for yourself?" Levant said. "You have a brain!"

"That *is* what I think!" Grace said, stomping off.

Grace loved reading all kinds of books. *Uncle Tom's Cabin*, one of the most popular novels of that time, deeply affected her.

"Slavery is wrong, Papa!" Grace exclaimed, showing him her book. "We don't have any slaves in Westfield, do we?"

"No," her father replied. "New York is a free state."

"Then I'm proud to live here," Grace said.

"If Abraham Lincoln is elected president this fall," her father said, "I think he'll end slavery throughout the whole country."

"I really hope he wins," Grace said.

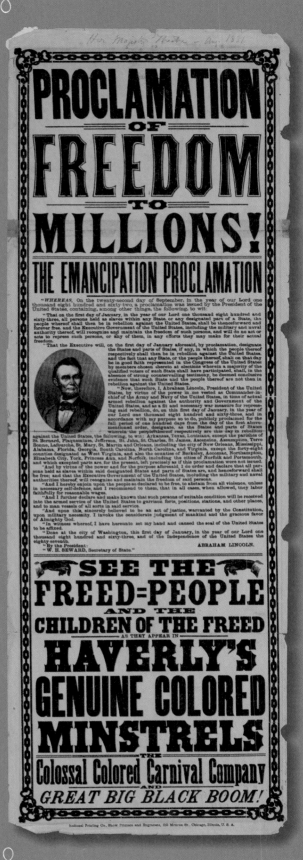

LINCOLN AND SLAVERY

When Abraham Lincoln became president, America was divided into "free" states, "slave" states, and territories. Since Lincoln's primary interest was in preserving the Union (keeping the United States together) he initially favored allowing the southern "slave" states to remain that way. He was, however, strongly against slavery extending into any more territories. This was land in the western part of the United States that had not yet become states. At this time, Lincoln was not an abolitionist, someone who thought slavery should be totally stopped everywhere. During the Civil War, Lincoln's position changed. On January 1, 1863, he issued an executive order, the Emancipation Proclamation, proclaiming that slaves who lived in the ten states that were still fighting against the North in the Civil War were now freed. In December 1865, the Thirteenth Amendment was passed. This made slavery illegal throughout all of the United States. Because Abraham Lincoln did so much to end slavery, many people refer to him as the "Great Emancipator."

When September arrived, it was time for school.

"Good-bye, Mother! Bye-bye, Una!" Grace said as she walked out the door. Born in August, Grace's baby sister, Eunice, was already one month old.

From his desk at the front of the classroom, Grace's teacher talked about Lincoln and Douglas, the two main presidential candidates.

During afternoon recess, the boys chased one another in a game of tag. Since it wasn't acceptable for girls to take part in active games during school, Grace and her friends played Cat's Cradle instead. While waiting for her turn, she overheard one of her classmates.

"Lincoln's so ugly," a boy said to his friend. "I can't believe he's running for president."

"He is *not* ugly!" Grace called out. "And he's going to be the best president *ever*!"

In October, Grace's father attended a hometown fair in support of Lincoln. Upon returning home in the evening, he had a surprise for Grace.

"It's a picture of Mr. Lincoln!" Grace said, holding up a campaign poster. "Thank you, Papa."

As Grace walked up the stairs to her bedroom, Levant called out, "He'll never become president with a face like that!"

"Yes, he will!" Grace said. She slammed the door behind her.

Moving to a chair by the window, Grace took a close look at Lincoln's face. She admired his high forehead and serious expression.

But I don't like the way his mouth and chin look, she thought.

A shadow fell across Lincoln's face. Grace had an idea.
"He would look much better with whiskers!" she
exclaimed.

On October 15, Grace sat at her desk and wrote a letter to Abraham Lincoln. She introduced herself and asked him if he had any daughters. Most importantly, she suggested, "... let your whiskers grow... for your face is so thin." Grace added that women like whiskers and "... they would tease their husbands to vote for you and then you would be president."

Grace dipped her pen into a bottle of ink and printed "Hon. Abraham Lincoln, Springfield, Illinois" on the envelope. She placed her letter inside, sealed it, and added a penny stamp. With a bounce in her step, she brought it to the post office.

If Mr. Lincoln answers my letter, Grace thought, *I'll certainly have something to show Levant.*

VOTES FOR WOMEN

WOMEN AND VOTING

Throughout most of Grace Bedell's life, women were not permitted to vote. The fight for women's suffrage (the right to vote) began in the 1820s. Many women of this time were discontent with the limitations put on them for earning money outside the home. They wanted the same rights and privileges as men. Women fought hard for equal rights during the 1800s and early 1900s. After World War I, women's contributions on behalf of the war effort helped change public opinion. Women were finally granted the right to vote on August 26, 1920, when the Nineteeth Amendment to the Constitution was passed. On Election Day 1920, when Grace Bedell was almost seventy-two years old, women voted in national and local elections for the very first time.

Suffragette Parade,
March 3, 1913

Flag of the National Women's Party Suffrage Movement

Later that same week, Abraham Lincoln sorted through his mail. He noticed an envelope that featured the unmistakable handwriting of a child.

Lincoln smiled as he read Grace's letter.

So, an eleven-year-old girl thinks I will increase my chances of getting elected if I let my whiskers grow, he thought. *Well, perhaps she's right!*

A few days later, Grace returned to the post office.
"Is there something for me?" Grace asked David Mann,
the postmaster. Everybody in Westfield knew Mr. Mann.
"Sorry, not today," the postmaster replied after a few
minutes.

She returned the next day and the day after that. Still nothing.

Finally, on October 22, Mr. Mann excitedly handed Grace a letter. "It's from Abraham Lincoln!" he announced.

"Mr. Lincoln answered my letter!" Grace cried out. "I can't believe it!"

Even though it was only October, a light snow was falling. Grace almost slipped as she ran home.

"Look what I've got, Mama!" Grace shouted as she burst through the door. "It's from Mr. Lincoln. He answered my letter!"

"Goodness gracious!" her mother replied. "I didn't even know you wrote to him."

"It was a secret," Grace explained. "Nobody knew but me."

Grace went to the parlor and found Levant.

"Look!" she shouted. "It's from Mr. Lincoln!"

"Why on earth would Abraham Lincoln write a letter to you?" Levant asked.

"Because I wrote to him first," Grace said. "And now he answered me."

"My, my," Levant said. "Lincoln actually wrote a letter to my little sister."

"Aren't you proud?" asked Grace's mother.

"Yes, I guess I am," Levant replied.

Grace ran upstairs and into her room. She was pleased with every word of Lincoln's letter . . . until she came to the last sentence. "As to the whiskers," he wrote, "do you not think people would call it a piece of silly affection if I were to begin it now?"

It sounds like Mr. Lincoln won't be growing whiskers, Grace thought sadly. *That's too bad. I thought I was right about that.*

The election took place on Tuesday, November 6, 1860. Grace was hoping with all her heart that Lincoln would be the next president.

When Grace finally heard the news that Lincoln had won, she jumped up and down with delight.

A few months later, on the morning of February 16, 1861, Grace woke up with the sun.

"Get out of bed, sleepyheads!" she said, shaking her two older sisters. "President Lincoln is stopping here on his way to Washington, DC. Remember?"

"Yes, of course," Helen said, rubbing her eyes. "But his train won't be arriving until later in the day."

"I know," Grace replied. "But let's get ready now!"

LINCOLN'S FIRST PRESIDENTIAL INAUGURATION

After Abraham Lincoln won the presidential election on November 6, 1860, he had a few weeks to put his affairs in order before traveling to Washington, DC, to give his first inaugural address. On February 11, 1861, Lincoln boarded a train in Springfield, Illinois. Making a few stops at different northern cities along the way – including Westfield, NY, to meet Grace Bedell – he arrived in Washington, DC, on February 23. In modern times, the president's inauguration is always at noon on January 20. When Lincoln was inaugurated, the date was March 4, to coincide with the date on which the Constitution of the United States took effect in 1789.

By the time Lincoln gave his address, seven states had already seceded from the Union and had formed the Confederate States of America. Despite this turn of events, Lincoln desperately wanted to keep the Union together and to avoid a war between the southern and northern states.

Inauguration of Abraham Lincoln, March 4, 1861

Along with Grace and her sisters, thousands of people converged at the Westfield train station, hoping to get a glimpse of the new president.

"I hope he has whiskers," Grace said.

When his train arrived, Lincoln stepped out of the last car to address the crowd. As he spoke, Grace stood on her tiptoes.

"There are too many people." Grace said. "I can't see him!"

"There he is!" Alice exclaimed. "And he *does* have whiskers."

"Really?" Grace said. "Let me see!"

After a short speech, Lincoln peered into a mass of people. "I have a little correspondent in this place," he announced, "and if she is present, will she please come forward?"

"Who is it?" shouted one of the spectators.

"Grace Bedell!" answered Lincoln.

The crowd parted and a man led Grace to Lincoln's train car. He stepped down and shook Grace's hand.

"You see," Lincoln said, pointing to his whiskers, "I let these grow for you, Grace."

A thunderous cheer filled the air as Lincoln kissed Grace's cheek and returned to his train car. He waved a US flag as the train pulled away.

Blushing with embarrassment, Grace rushed to get away from the train station. Racing between horses and buggies, and even crawling under a lumber wagon, she left her sisters and ran all the way home.

"I can't believe it!" Grace breathlessly told her mother. "Abraham Lincoln wanted to meet me! And he *did* grow whiskers, just like I asked him to!"

"What a story!" Grace's mother said.

"This is the most exciting day of my life!" Grace said. "I can't wait to tell Papa!"

Hon A B Lincoln

Dear Sir

My father has just home from the fair and brought home your picture and Mr. Hamlin's. I am a little girl only eleven years old, but want you should be President of the United States very much so I hope you wont think me very bold to write to such a great man as you are. Have you any little girls about as large as I am if so give them my love and tell her to write to me if you cannot answer this letter. I have got 4 brother's and part of them will vote for you any way and if you let your whiskers grow I will try and get the rest of them to vote for you you would look a great deal better for your face is so thin. All the ladies like whiskers and they would tease their husband's to vote for you and then you would be President. My father is going to vote for you and if I was a man I would vote for you to but I will try to get every one to vote for you that I can I think that rail fence around your picture makes it look very pretty I have got a little baby sister she is nine weeks old and is just as cunning as can be. When you direct your letter direct to Grace Bedell Westfield Chatauque County New York.

I must not write any more answer this letter right off Good bye

Grace Bedell

Miss Grace Bedell

My dear little Miss.

Your very agreeable letter of the 15th is received —

I regret the necessity of saying I have no daughters.

I have three sons — one seventeen, one nine, and one seven years of age. They, with their mother, constitute my whole family —

As to the whiskers, having never worn any, do you not think people would call it a piece of silly affection if I were to begin it now?

Your very sincere well wisher

A. Lincoln

BEGINNING OF THE CIVIL WAR

Although Abraham Lincoln won the 1860 presidential election, he did not win any of the southern states. By the time Lincoln took office, the Confederacy was established and functioning. Two days after Lincoln's inauguration, the Confederate government called for 100,000 men for its new army. At about the same time, Confederate officials in Charleston, South Carolina, demanded the surrender of Union-held Fort Sumter. The commander, Major Robert Anderson, refused to surrender. Supplies were running out. Lincoln notified the authorities that he planned to send additional soldiers and supplies to the fort. On April 12, 1861, South Carolina's militia forces opened fire on Fort Sumter. The Civil War had begun.

GRACE BEDELL'S LATER LIFE

In 1867, at the age of 19, Grace Bedell married George Billings, a Civil War soldier who fought for the North. They courageously picked up their roots in Westfield, NY, and, not sure what would happen to them, moved out west. They settled in Delphos, Kansas, and lived difficult pioneer lives. When they started, their only possessions were a small home and a team of oxen. As a pioneer woman, Grace made feed-sack curtains for the windows and mended clothes. When it rained, she struggled to keep the rainwater from coming in through the door. Beef jerky and cornbread were examples of the food they ate. Grace Billings died on November 2, 1936, in Delphos, at the age of 87. In the 1990s, the letter that Grace wrote to Lincoln when she was eleven years old was placed on sale for a price of $1,000,000.

THE STATUE OF GRACE BEDELL AND ABRAHAM LINCOLN

In July 1999, a statue of Grace Bedell and Abraham Lincoln was unveiled in Westfield, New York. It commemorated the meeting of Lincoln and Grace after the presidential election of 1860. It shows the wonderful anticipation of a young girl's meeting with arguably our greatest president, Abraham Lincoln. The letters between Grace and Lincoln are also engraved on a monument in Delphos, Kansas, where Grace lived as an adult. The inscription on the monument reads: "Delphos: The Home of Lincoln's Little Correspondent."